DANNY ORLIS *and the* SKI SLOPE EMERGENCY

by

BERNARD PALMER

MOODY PRESS

CHICAGO

ISBN: 0-8024-7242-7

Printed in the United States of America

DANNY ORLIS *and the* SKI SLOPE EMERGENCY

Contents

1

Party Plans

DeeDee Davis tossed her shining black hair from her eyes with a quick, defiant movement of her head and turned to Kay Orlis.

"I know it's the Christian thing for me to be friends with Letitia, but it simply does no good to even try. I don't think she wants to be friends with anybody."

"I thought she was your friend," Kay replied mildly.

DeeDee walked slowly across the kitchen and sat down across from her foster mother. "I guess we're friends, in a way. But I was thinking about being closer than just speaking to each other in school and having lunch together once in awhile. Sandy and I were really close friends. We shared our problems with each other and cheered each other up if we were down."

"I know what you mean. A close friend is really important."

"I've tried and tried to get close to Letitia, but I think I'm wasting my time. She talks to me about what's going on at school or church, but she never says anything about herself. She won't mention how she feels or what's happening at home. Most of the time I think I don't even know her."

Kay listened understandingly, but she had little advice to offer. DeeDee really hadn't expected her to offer the perfect solution. It was just good to have someone to talk to even though the situation did seem hopeless.

She didn't know why she promised Hank that she would try to help his sister. Of course things were better now. For a while Letitia wouldn't even talk to DeeDee. Now, at least, they were on friendly terms. Still, the barriers were there. Letitia would allow DeeDee to get just so close and that was all.

"Hank thinks I should ask Letitia to go to the youth party at church next week."

"Are you going to?"

DeeDee sighed. "I told him I would, but now I wish I hadn't. She won't go."

"You won't know that until you've tried."

DeeDee raised her head. Her dark eyes flashed. "That's what Hank said, but you wait and see.

She's *never* gone anywhere I've asked her to. This time won't be any different."

"I'll be praying for you, DeeDee, and for Letitia, too."

DeeDee's annoyance disappeared. "Thanks," she said. "I'll need it."

She found Letitia Warren in the crowded hall at school the next morning and managed to get her out of the relentless crush long enough to ask her about going to the party. Just as she expected, Letitia's face darkened and she seemed to shrink away.

"I don't like parties very well," was Letitia's lame excuse.

"But you'll like this one!"

"Thanks anyway, DeeDee," she said distantly, "but I don't think I'm interested."

DeeDee was sure Letitia did not mean what she said. Everybody liked parties, especially the ones at church. She still thought Fairview was better in every way than Rock Point, but she had to admit the parties at their new church were more fun than any she had ever gone to.

"Have you ever been to one of the church parties?" DeeDee persisted.

"A couple of times," Letitia answered. It was obvious that she did not like to be pressured.

"Didn't you have a good time?"

"They were all right, I guess, if there was nothing else to do," Letitia replied.

DeeDee would have stopped then but she had promised Hank she would do everything she could to get his sister to go to the party. "Why don't you go to this party with me and give them another chance? Maybe the ones you went to weren't too much, but you ought to try them now. Everybody has a ball!"

"I'll see," Letitia answered defensively, as though she only agreed to that much in order to get DeeDee to stop pressing her.

"We can't wait any longer. If we're going, we'll have to sign up right away."

Finally she agreed to go, but with obvious reluctance.

"I'll sign up," she said, "but I don't think I'll have much fun."

DeeDee should have felt good about getting Letitia to agree to go to the party with her, but she was doubtful.

"I'm still afraid she'll back out," she told Hank.

"You did your best," Hank said, grinning. "That's all anybody can do."

DeeDee's brother, Doug, was thinking about another kind of a party, however. Tina Nicholson, the blond vision of loveliness who lived next door, invited him to go skiing with her and her family the next day. There was fresh snow in the hills, making the runs fast and exciting.

"Mother and Daddy are going up to the hills to our cabin to do some work and they said I could ask you to go along."

"Sounds great."

"Be sure to bring your skis," she reminded him.

Doug laughed. It was not so long ago that he would not have dared to accept an invitation that required him to bring along his skis. He still was not as proficient as he wanted to be, but he could manage to stay on his feet and negotiate the average slope without taking a chance on breaking a leg or knocking someone else off the mountain. Besides, the basketball season had just ended, and it was fun to have another sport to enjoy.

"Maybe I can enjoy skiing this time," he told her.

They left Rock Point for the Nicholson cabin before daylight that Saturday morning and in half an hour they were unstrapping their skis from the top of the car.

"This is a beautiful day!" Tina exclaimed as she pulled herself erect and pivoted slowly to survey the beauty of the early morning lights and shadows.

"And the snow is perfect. It's going to be marvelous skiing."

She was right about the snow. There was a fresh layer of powder that made the skiing almost perfect. The still air and the warm sun made the day just right. They had a great time on the mountain.

After a couple of hesitant trips down the run, Doug felt his confidence and skill building. He scarcely thought about falling anymore; and when he did, much of the fear was gone. Tina noticed the improvement in his skill and complimented him for it.

"You're going to be a great skier, Doug."

"Yeh, if I can stay alive that long," he answered flippantly.

"Don't be silly. You really are good, considering how little experience you've had."

"Oh sure. The next thing you know, they'll be holding a place for me on the Olympic team."

In spite of his own dim view of his ability, by midafternoon Doug was able to race down the slope at Tina's side.

As they climbed back up the hill after their last run Tina mentioned that she was planning a skiing party.

"Do you think the kids would like to come up

here for a day of skiing a couple of weeks after the party at church?" she asked.

"They'd have to be out of their minds if they didn't."

"Daddy said I could have a party some Saturday and invite the kids from church."

"You can't beat that," Doug said enthusiastically.

Tina was so excited about the ski party that she set to work immediately, making plans for it. "I'm going to ask DeeDee to help me," Tina mentioned. "She seems to have lots of good ideas. And, of course, I hope you'll help too, Doug."

Doug did not feel enthusiastic about working with DeeDee; but now that she and Tina had become friends, it would be all wrong to object.

"I'll ask DeeDee to meet us after school Monday to talk about it. You can be there, can't you, Doug?"

He gazed in her direction. "And if I can't?" he asked, trying to see how solidly DeeDee was in with Tina.

"Then I guess the two of us could take care of things."

The frown lines about his mouth deepened. He guessed it would be best to work with DeeDee without complaining. She was not such a bad sister anyway.

DeeDee was gateful for the opportunity to help Tina plan for the ski party. It made it seem more like old times back in Fairview. She and Sandy had been in on most of the parties their circle of friends had given. She had forgotten how much she missed it.

DeeDee had all but forgotten about the church party until Hank ate lunch with her the day before it was to be held.

"Well, you were right," he said glumly.

"About what?"

"Letitia. She's decided she isn't going to the party tomorrow night."

"I'm not surprised," DeeDee replied despondently.

Hank asked hesitantly, "You don't suppose it would do any good to ask her again, do you?"

"It wouldn't do me any good. I said everything I could think of to get her to agree to go with me when I talked to her. There isn't anything more I could say now." DeeDee grinned crookedly, knowing Hank had a date the following evening. "Why don't you ask Letitia to go with you?"

His lean face flushed. "You know why."

"Don't you think Betty would like having you bring your sister along?"

"Are you kidding? I don't even think she wants to go to a church party."

Knowing Betty, DeeDee thought Hank was right.

The party was even more successful than previous ones had been but it was dampened somewhat for DeeDee by Letitia's refusal to come. However, she had not asked her about going again. She had given up.

In fact, for a couple of days after the party DeeDee did not even try to see Letitia. DeeDee was not angry, but she decided she would rather not continue such a cold friendship. She liked Letitia as much as ever and still longed to be closer to her, but it seemed that Letitia would rather be alone.

On Wednesday of the following week, however, Letitia met DeeDee at her locker after school. "I'm sorry I didn't go to the party with you," she said.

"That's all right."

"I hope you're not mad at me."

DeeDee's smile was reassuring. "I did feel bad about it, but that was only because I thought you had decided you didn't want to be with me anymore and I do want to have you for a friend."

Letitia looked confused and troubled. "That's not the way it is at all," she stammered. "I count you as my very best friend. I didn't see you after deciding not to go to the party because I figured you didn't want to be with me. Nobody else does."

DeeDee saw that her lips were trembling and detected a helpless note in her voice. "That's not true, Letitia," she said firmly. "Everybody likes you."

Letitia was not ready to believe that.

"You're just saying that because you feel sorry for me and want to make me feel better," she said. "I don't know what's the matter with me. Everybody avoids me."

DeeDee tried to get her to understand that she was liked as well as anyone else in the junior class, but she would not listen. She continued to protest that nothing anyone said to her would make her feel differently. At last, in desperation, DeeDee changed the subject.

2

Letitia's Theme

After that encounter Letitia treated DeeDee with new warmth and respect. It seemed as though she had finally become aware of the fact that DeeDee honestly wanted to be her friend. She waited by her locker for her to come to school in the morning and usually managed to eat lunch with her at noon. They had the same study period every afternoon and went into the library where they worked on their latest, and most important, English theme together.

As usual, Letitia was sure she would do a poor job and that she was going to get a failing grade.

"I don't see why we get assignments like this," she complained. "I'll flunk it for sure. And Miss Arvidson said it's the most important assignment of the year."

DeeDee held the same uneasy feeling about her own half-finished theme. She had never been good at writing but she dare not say anything to Letitia about her fears. That would make Letitia all the more unsure of her own efforts than she was already.

"No matter how hard I try, DeeDee, it doesn't come out right. I might as well give up."

"You can't do that," DeeDee whispered. "You've got to finish it. You can't just take a zero for the assignment. You'll never bring up your grade."

"But it's no use. I can never write the rest of this theme to suit her. I'm going to throw it away."

DeeDee snatched the four pages from Letitia's hand.

"DeeDee, don't waste your time reading that!" Letitia objected.

The librarian was glaring at the girls. They stopped talking and DeeDee read Letitia's paper to herself. She was amazed. It was really good. The description sparkled and the writing itself was vivid and expertly paced. There was an easy flow to the words that set the mood for the entire piece. It had a poetic quality.

DeeDee scribbled a note to Letitia that said: "This theme is beautiful! Miss Arvidson will flip! What are you worried about? This makes my paper sound like *The Three Little Pigs.*"

Letitia glanced at the note, then she opened her notebook and took out three more pages. Handing them to Dee Dee she said quietly, "I didn't know if I should hand in that theme or this one."

DeeDee took the pages, marvelling that Letitia would allow her to read something else she had written. Letitia seemed to want to take the theme back after she offered it but the librarian was staring in their direction again. She sat solemnly while DeeDee read.

The theme was completely different. The writing was just as good, but it was more of a character sketch or a short story about a girl their own age.

The character, Susan, was so upset she was seriously thinking about taking her own life. No one loved her. Her parents had not wanted her when she was born. She had caused them all sorts of problems and put them in debt. She had been ill and she suspected that her mother's health had been endangered by her birth.

Susan had never brought anything but trouble to anyone who associated with her, and now she had reached the place where life held nothing for her anymore. She decided that suicide would be a favor to her family.

DeeDee shuddered.

Letitia leaned forward slightly, unsure of what to say. "What do you think about it?" she asked. "Do you like it?"

"It's beautifully written," DeeDee acknowledged, "but—"

Letitia took it back and tore the pages in half, impulsively. "That's what I was afraid of. I knew I wasn't getting it the way I wanted it. I knew it wouldn't come off."

"It's not that at all. If you want the truth, it came off so well it disturbed me. As I read it I got the feeling that I wasn't reading a story, I was looking into the life of a real person. I felt as though I was intruding where I shouldn't have."

Letitia's gaze seemed to be reaching out for DeeDee in desperation, but only for an instant. She shrunk within herself, like a turtle pulling into its shell.

Letitia scribbled a note to DeeDee to avoid getting shushed again. "The next time I'll write about a pretty little rich girl who never has any problems. How would that suit you?"

"Better than what I read," DeeDee answered truthfully.

Letitia seemed to be so happy after school that DeeDee was sure she had been mistaken about the story and that everything was all right. The feeling that she had been reading her friend's innermost thoughts ebbed slowly away. When she got home, however, snatches of the story came to mind and the same fears rushed back. The theme was so vivid, so penetrating, it made her heart ache for Susan. Or was it Letitia? Was she trying to tell something about herself that she did not quite dare identify as her own problem?

DeeDee knew it was ridiculous for her to feel so melancholy about a story but the more she went over it in her mind the more upset she became.

She would have liked to take Kay into her confidence and ask her advice but there was nothing to tell her that she was sure about. And the idea persisted that to tell anyone about the story would have been violating her friend's confidence.

At DeeDee's insistence, Letitia retyped the theme she had torn up and handed it in. She got an A plus on it. Miss Arvidson even read it to the class and said she was going to keep it and submit it to a high school magazine.

"This is one of the best pieces of work I have seen in my years of teaching high school English. It deserves far more recognition than we are able to give it here."

Letitia's cheeks bloomed crimson and she squirmed under the admiring stares of her classmates. When the class was over she told DeeDee about her embarrassment. "I don't think I've ever felt so awful in my life. I wanted to fall right through the floor."

"Awful?" DeeDee echoed. "You should have been honored. That's the way Miss Arvidson meant you to take what she said. She was complimenting you."

"But I felt so silly. I didn't know what to say."

During the next week DeeDee was so involved with helping Tina plan her ski party that she did not give too much thought to Letitia and her problems. As the time for the party approached, however, she realized she should contact her friend to be sure that she was going.

She tried to see her at school that day, but was not able to find her. She even waited in the hall until everyone else had gone into the lunch room in the hope that she would show up, but she was nowhere around. The only thing she could think of was that Letitia was ill.

I'll phone her when I get home and see how she is, if I don't see Hank around the school building so I can ask him, DeeDee decided.

When she got home she phoned the Warren home. She half expected Letitia to answer, but it was her mother on the line.

"I'll see if Letitia is able to talk right now," she said hesitantly, as though there was some question in her mind as to whether or not her daughter would be able to come to the phone. That, in itself, was disturbing to DeeDee. If Letitia was ill her mother would know whether or not she could come to the phone.

"Is she ill?" DeeDee really had not meant to ask that. The question popped out unexpectedly.

"She doesn't feel too well." There was a strangely taut tone in the woman's voice. "If you'll wait a moment I'll go and talk to her."

It was a long while before Letitia answered, and when she did there was a tightness in her voice that DeeDee could not quite understand.

"Your mother said you weren't feeling well. I hope you'll be better soon."

"I'm all right," Letitia murmured.

"I'm glad to hear that. Tina and I were concerned about you. We looked for you in school today but we didn't see you."

There was no answer.

"You remember I talked with you about the skiing party Saturday, don't you?"

"Yes."

"What time should I come over and pick you up?"

Letitia coughed nervously. "I don't think I'll be

able to go, after all." A queer little sob choked off the sentence.

"Letitia! Are you all right?" DeeDee demanded. She could hear Letitia sobbing uncontrollably.

"I'm sorry," she managed after a time. "I can't talk any more right now." Then she hung up.

DeeDee sat quietly, her thoughts churning. There was something most disturbing about Letitia Warren. DeeDee had felt it since the first time Hank asked her to befriend his sister. Of late the feeling had grown markedly. Now she realized it was a far more serious problem than she had even suspected. And the worst of it was there was nothing she could do about it!

3

Ski Party

DEEDEE WENT BACK to her studies but she could not stop thinking about Letitia. She claimed to be a Christian and DeeDee had no reason to doubt her, although at first she thought that was the problem. But Letitia's testimony sounded clear. She told her about having made a decision for Christ when she was seven years old, and how she tried to live for Him. Still, she was overwhelmed by some problem that darkened all her thinking.

After trying to study for half an hour DeeDee closed her book suddenly. She felt that she had to go over to see Letitia, at least for a little while. She had to find out if there was something she could do to help. She went to Danny, explained the situation and asked to borrow the car.

"I feel as though I've got to go over and see what's bothering her so much," she said. "Letitia's awfully upset about something."

Danny nodded and gave DeeDee the keys. He

was glad that DeeDee had taken such an interest in Letitia because he knew her problems were serious.

When DeeDee arrived at the Warren home some fifteen or twenty minutes later, she found Letitia in a more despondent mood than ever. She greeted DeeDee and invited her in. The house was clean but the carpet was badly worn and a spring in the threadbare couch poked up through one of the cushions. Letitia's face was somber and her eyes were red from crying.

"I was so worried about you I felt that I had to come over and talk to you, Letitia," DeeDee explained.

"I'm all right," Letitia said weakly as she motioned DeeDee to a chair.

DeeDee's gaze held hers. "I don't think you are all right. You were crying so hard when I talked with you a little while ago that I couldn't help being concerned."

Letitia's cheeks flushed darkly. "It really isn't much of anything. It's nothing you can do anything about, anyway."

DeeDee stared at her. "Sometimes it helps just to talk things out. I know when I feel blue and discouraged, just sharing my problems with someone else makes me feel better."

Letitia hesitated. A certain longing crept into her eyes.

"I don't want to burden you with my troubles, but I've got to talk to somebody," she blurted. "Dad got laid off yesterday and it doesn't look as though he'll be able to go back to work at his old job for a long time. The company is making a lot of changes. They may never need him again."

"Oh, that's too bad," DeeDee sympathized, not really knowing what to say.

Letitia gestured helplessly. "And that's not all. He doesn't know where he's going to be able to get another job."

DeeDee murmured her regrets. She knew what she was saying was trite and not the least bit helpful, but she did not know what else to say.

"This isn't the first time it's happened." Now that she was talking the words tumbled out in such a torrent that at times DeeDee had difficulty in understanding her. "It seems as though Dad can never find a job that really suits him, or if he does, something like this happens. It's always been that way."

DeeDee stared at her friend with new desperation in her face. She had been anxious to have Letitia talk to her before. Now that she had, she was bewildered and uncertain as to what she should do or say. What could she tell her that would help at a time like this?

"I don't know what to say or do, Letitia," she confessed flatly. "Nothing I could say would help because I've never been in a situation like you and your family are in. But God knows and understands. Why don't we ask Him to help?"

Letitia's expression grew even more sullen and despondent. "I used to think that praying helped. I don't any more. I've prayed and prayed, but nothing's changed! God doesn't even hear me!"

Tears flooded her eyes. "You'd better go now, DeeDee. Thank you for coming over to talk."

DeeDee reluctantly said good-bye and had her hand on the door when she remembered the skiing party.

"Oh, I wanted to ask you about Tina's party again," DeeDee added, "You're going to be able to go with me, aren't you?"

Letitia frowned. "I don't know. Right now I don't feel much like going to a party."

"I'll be praying for you," DeeDee said. "I'll pray that your father gets the right job and that you will be able to go to the party."

For the next few days, the late February weather brought no additional accumulation of snow. Tina and the others made final plans for the ski party on

Saturday. And again DeeDee talked with Letitia about going. At first Letitia refused, saying she was not a good skier and would not have any fun. At DeeDee's insistence, however, she finally agreed to go.

"You'll have a good time. I can tell you that right now," DeeDee assured her.

Letitia shrugged indifferently, as though she felt herself above and beyond parties and skiing. This time, though, she did not call to back out as she had before. That made DeeDee happy.

"If we can just get her out to one of our parties, I'm sure she'll want to go to all the rest of them," DeeDee told the family on Friday night.

"Nobody will have as much fun as Doug," Del teased. "He loves to go skiing at the Nicholson's for some reason."

"Lay off, will you?" Doug complained.

"I just made a simple observation. I'm not going to tell anybody you've been so excited about going to this party that you've hardly slept all week, or that you keep mumbling in your sleep about cadillacs."

Doug's glare told Del that he had said enough.

The following morning four cars took the kids up to the mountain cabin Tina's folks owned. Letitia was the last to get to the Nicholson home in

Rock Point before the group left. In fact DeeDee was beginning to get concerned that she might not be coming at all. But she arrived just moments before Mr. Nicholson announced that it was time to leave.

As soon as they reached the cabin Del and Doug helped Mr. Nicholson unload the snowmobiles from the trailer and build a fire in the fireplace. The cabin was warm, and the fire just made the atmosphere more friendly. They decided that it would be an excellent place to gather for devotions at noon.

The others were already on their skis. Everyone, that is, except Letitia. She had taken her skis and had gone over to the place where the others were getting ready to go down the slope. She stood alone, managing to look miserable, but without making a move to put on the skis herself. Del saw that she was alone and went over to her.

"Hi," he said.

She eyed him curiously and felt her cheeks glow. She had never noticed him before, but she thought he looked handsome that morning.

"Hello."

"All set to ski?"

"I don't know. I'm not exactly the most graceful thing on skis. I guess that's why I've been standing here. I haven't been able to make up my mind whether I ought to try it or not."

"But you've got to ski," he said firmly. "You can't come all this distance to spend the day in the cabin."

"But I haven't even been on skis yet this year."

He laughed again, bringing a smile to her face. "Don't feel so bad about that. I hadn't even been on skis until we moved out here so I don't ski well at all. The chances are I'll fall and break my neck before I've gone a dozen yards. Now what do you think of that?"

Letitia could not believe that he was telling her the truth. Everybody around Rock Point knew how to ski, even the tiniest children. Everyone else she knew could ski a lot better than she could. "You don't expect me to believe that, do you?" she asked.

"I'm telling you the truth." Del talked easily with her, as if she were his sister. "We had plenty of snow back in Minnesota where we used to live, but we didn't have the hills so we didn't have a chance to learn to ski." He paused. "Some of the guys would go to the eastern part of the state and ski once in awhile but it sure isn't the big deal it is around here. And falling isn't such a big deal, either."

Del had surprised himself by even going over to talk with Letitia. He certainly hadn't planned on it. He hadn't even planned on it when he saw her standing alone while the other kids were getting ready for the slopes. It was one of those things that just seemed to happen.

Before long Del was helping Letitia with her skis. He surprised himself. She was too shy to ask him to help. But there he was, helping her into her ski boots just like Doug had done for Tina. He was just finishing the job when Doug glanced in his direction and saw what he was doing.

"Hey, Del!" There was a taunting tone in his voice. "What're you doing?"

The color crept up into Del's cheeks to the root of his dark hair. For a moment he was flustered.

"Del! I didn't know you were so interested in helping."

Letitia could not quite understand what was going on. It put Del in an uncomfortable position. He tried to explain so that Letitia would not feel they were joking about her. It made him a little sorry that he had teased Doug so much about Tina.

Del only spent a few minutes with Letitia before skiing away. He did not really want to leave her alone. It was sort of fun being with a girl like her. And he probably could have helped her some.

DeeDee kept talking about how much she needed friends. But Doug would never let him be friendly to her without making a big deal out of it, he stormed inwardly.

Del did ski with Letitia a couple of times during the day, when he was sure that Doug was nowhere around. He thought Letitia was cute and she seemed to enjoy being with him. Before the day was over he had decided he was going to ask her out once in a while, if she would go with him, and if he could sneak away from Doug long enough.

The party was a terrific success. Tina's folks had their snowmobiles at the cabin and when the kids got tired of skiing they took them on the power toboggans, racing up the game trails and over the deep snow. Everyone was sorry when the sun began to set and it was time to go home.

Doug and Del helped Mr. Nicholson load the snowmobiles on the trailer while the other guys started loading the cars with equipment. Suddenly a shrill, terrified scream sounded from the ski slope.

Everyone jerked erect, conversation choking in their throats momentarily. Then they all ran to the slopes to investigate.

4

Emergency!

A SECOND PIERCING SCREECH of pain sounded in the still winter air, driving terror to the very marrow of their bones.

A row of trees screened the ski run from view. The two guys who got to the edge of the slope first shouted back, "It's Letitia! Letitia Warren!"

Soon everyone who had arrived at the slope was talking and shouting at once. There, some two hundred yards or more below, lay Letitia's crumpled form.

Hank Warren, who had been fastening skis to the rack on top of one of the cars, dropped the strap he was holding and charged after Tina's dad in the direction of the ski run, almost colliding with Doug. At first the trees and people blocked his view. The viselike bands of dread tightened about Hank's chest until he fought to breathe.

"Letitia!" He shouted. His anguished cry echoed

across the mountain as he looked down in unbelief at his injured sister.

A sudden icy spasm gripped Del's stomach and squeezed relentlessly. Letitia was so still and motionless he wondered at first if she was still alive. Then he thought he saw her stir slightly.

Mr. Nicholson, who had been on the National Ski Patrol when he was younger, had paused only an instant before runnning and sliding down the ski run to the place where she was lying. Quickly he bent over her.

"Letitia," he said firmly, but without a trace of fear or panic.

She groaned but did not answer him.

"Letitia!" He cried again, louder this time. In spite of himself his voice broke.

Doug, Del and Hank were the next to reach the place where the injured girl lay. They were followed an instant or two later by the others, who eyed her wordlessly. The shock of seeing her lying there so still and quiet was enough to force them to silence.

DeeDee, who was a bit slower to reach Letitia than the others, pushed through the tense crowd to stand beside Del and Doug, looking down at her injured friend. She, too, was caught in the hush of the moment. She felt dizzy and shivered violently.

Letitia did not move for a matter of some seconds and DeeDee wondered if she was able to. She ached within to think how seriously she must be hurt. Then, when it seemed that Letitia would never move again, her eyelids fluttered slightly and an arm jerked.

DeeDee caught a quick breath. "Is—" she began, only to stop and with difficulty start again. "Is she hurt seriously?"

"She seems to be regaining consciousness," Mr. Nicholson said, unable to tell them anything about the girl's condition. He turned back to the twisted form on the snow, hoping the kids had not noticed the look of worry on his face or caught the concern that had been in his voice.

Letitia's left arm was twisted at a grotesque angle, and she had a limp rag doll look. Since he reached her side, she had been lying almost completely motionless. There was no way of knowing, at this point, whether she was seriously hurt or not.

It could be that she had suffered a comparatively minor injury. That often was the case in skiing accidents. There were plenty of sprained ankles and broken legs and arms and few accidents worse. But there were some serious ones, some fatal injuries.

Something had to be done immediately without making the injury worse than it was already.

"Del," Mr. Nicholson said crisply, "take a couple of guys up to the cabin and bring back all the blankets you can find. We've got to keep her as warm as possible."

Del obeyed immediately, glad to have something to do besides standing there helplessly.

"And you, Doug, take one of the cars and get down to a phone as quickly as you can and call the ambulance. Tell them we've got to have them up here on the double."

"Will do." Doug turned and half ran up the slope. He had gone no more than a dozen paces when Mr. Nicholson sent Tina with him.

"Doug doesn't know the road too well!" he exclaimed. "And we don't want to take a chance on his getting lost. You'd better go along and show him the way."

She did as she was told. They were halfway up the slope when her dad called to them again. "Better tell the hospital to send a doctor along with that ambulance!"

"There's something I can't understand about this whole mess," Doug explained to Tina as they sped to the phone. Concern made his voice harsh. "Why did Letitia have to go out on that ski run just when we were leaving? She can't ski all that well and she doesn't even like to ski. I don't get it."

"I was thinking the same thing, myself," Tina commented. "She had to pick the steepest and most dangerous slope in this part of the hills. And anyone who's lived here very long knows that even the best skiers get in trouble on it."

"The way I got it, she's afraid of skiing."

"That's what she told DeeDee and me." There was a long pause. "She sure didn't have any business trying that run."

"I guess she knows that now."

Doug felt the car slide on a sharp corner and slowed down. Sliding off the mountain road now would complicate matters beyond belief. Just thinking about Letitia going on that ski run made him so angry that he had forgotten to be careful.

He had been watching the girl off and on that afternoon. She spent most of the time on the easy slopes, and it was easy to see that she had trouble enough taking care of herself there. He could not understand why she would pick the steepest slope in the whole area for her final trip down.

"This probably doesn't sound very kind," he said, "but it looks to me as though she almost wanted to get hurt."

Tina spoke up quickly. "Oh, I don't know, Doug. Maybe she just didn't know which run she was on."

Doug admitted that was possible. What Tina said made a lot more sense than what he was thinking. Nobody in her right mind would want to get hurt.

Back at the Nicholson cabin Del and Hank and a couple of other guys brought all the blankets they could find down to the place where Letitia lay motionless in the snow. Mr. Nicholson covered her with several blankets, taking great care not to move her as he did so. DeeDee still had not moved from her side.

"Is she conscious?" she asked tautly. She knew the answer to her question, even before she voiced it, but she felt that she had to say something to show her own concern.

Mr. Nicholson shook his head. He knew how the kids felt and tried to find something to ease their own fears without lying. "She's been drifting in and out of consciousness, I think," he said. "It's probably good that she isn't conscious now. She's probably in shock and in quite a lot of pain. The doctor will be here in a few minutes."

DeeDee pulled herself erect, tearing her gaze from Letitia's frail, twisted form for a moment. She was the one who had asked Letitia to come to the party. She had even begged her to come. This never would have happened to her if she had allowed her to stay at home.

She looked down at her friend once more, her gaze drawn back by some irresistible force. Staring at Letitia, she tried to pray. But there were times when it was almost impossible to find words to voice her anguish to God.

DeeDee did not know how long she had stood there, but presently Mrs. Nicholson came over and put an arm about her shoulder.

"We have to keep our trust in God," she said. "Don't worry about Letitia. He'll take care of her." Her voice was calm and reassuring.

"I know." DeeDee answered, tears coursing down her cheeks. And she did know that God would take care of her friend. Her trust was firm. ""But I feel so bad about the accident I can hardly stand it." She looked up. "You see, I'm the one who talked Letitia into coming to the party this morning."

"You can't blame yourself for what happened. You didn't know she was going out on the ski run and fall. That isn't the reason you asked her to join us." She paused for a time. "If you're going to reason that way, then Don and I have to assume the blame. We're the ones who should feel badly. We gave the party."

"It isn't your fault," DeeDee countered loyally.

"I know it isn't. And it isn't your fault, either."

"But why did it have to happen?"

"I can't answer that. There are times when God permits things like this to happen for His own purpose. We just have to trust Him that this accident is His will."

The silence was heavy between them.

"Why don't you take the kids up to the cabin and pray for Letitia?" Mrs. Nicholson suggested. "Don and I will stay here and look after her."

DeeDee began to say that she had to stay with Letitia, when she realized how foolish that would be. She could help more by praying than by standing in the cold doing nothing.

The others welcomed the opportunity to be doing something. They all went up to the cabin and knelt to pray. Some of the girls were crying when they began, but as they talked to God they quieted. It was not long until they were calm and resting in God's promises to hear and answer their prayers.

They were still on their knees when Doug and Tina drove into the open space before the cabin half an hour later. DeeDee got to her feet and ran out to meet them.

"Did you get the doctor?" she demanded.

"The ambulance will be here in a few minutes," Doug assured her.

Tina and Doug joined the others on their knees and continued to pray until the ambulance arrived and the doctor and the attendants rushed down to where Letitia was lying. The prayer meeting ended abruptly and everyone swarmed after the medical crew.

Mr. Nicholson stepped aside when he saw the doctor.

"You didn't move her, did you?" the doctor charged.

Mr. Nicholson assured him, "She's lying right where she fell."

"Good." He knelt to examine her swiftly.

Not until he finished did anyone speak.

"How is she?" Mr. Nicholson asked at last.

"She's got a badly injured back," the doctor replied. "I was afraid of that when I saw how she was lying. It's a very good thing she wasn't moved."

"Is it serious?" Mr. Nicholson kept his voice low, but in spite of that the kids heard him.

"We'll have to give a final answer to that question when we get her back to the hospital and take some X-rays, but as far as I can tell now, it's very serious."

5

Long Wait

RIDING BACK to Rock Point was an endless ordeal for DeeDee. All she could think about was her injured friend and the fact that she had been the one who urged Letitia to go to the ski party. Despite Mrs. Nicholson's reassurance, DeeDee continued to feel guilty. She tried to pray, but she was so distraught it seemed impossible.

DeeDee was not the only one who was thinking so much about Letitia on the way home. No one else talked much, either.

It was an hour after the group got back to town before they learned the full extent of Letitia's injuries. Don Nicholson and his wife were in the waiting room with Mr. and Mrs. Warren when the doctor came out to talk to Letitia's parents.

"How is she, Doctor?" Mrs. Warren asked as she hurried over to him, her voice thin and taut.

He was slow and deliberate in his reply. "You don't know how badly I hate to have to tell you this, but she has a broken arm and two broken vertabrae in her back."

"Oh, no!" The cry was of shock and disbelief.

Mr. Warren grasped his wife's hand and squeezed it tightly, but he did not speak. It was as though he could not.

"Fortunately, no one moved her until we got there," the doctor continued, "so the injury wasn't complicated by that. We have a fighting chance."

"What does that mean?" Mr. Warren demanded, brokenly.

"Just what I said, Mr. Warren. We can't make any promises about the outcome, but she's young and in good health and she wasn't hurt by being moved."

When DeeDee and Tina, who were also waiting in the lobby of the hospital for some word, heard the seriousness of Letitia's injuries, they both broke into tears. They had been sure that she was seriously injured by the way Mr. Nicholson took care of her and the fact that she had been unconscious, but they had not realized that her life was actually in danger.

As soon as Danny and Kay learned about the accident, they went down to the hospital. They really could not say that they knew the Warrens but they had met them casually on a couple of occasions.

At the hospital Danny and Kay talked with the Warrens for a few minutes, prayed with them, and urged Tina and DeeDee to come home with them. DeeDee didn't think she could stand to leave until she learned how Letitia was doing after they started to treat her.

"I've just got to stay and see how she gets along," she protested.

"Her folks are here," Kay told her, "and there's nothing you or anyone else, except the doctors, can do right now."

"But she may come to and ask for me. If she does I want to be here."

"I think you'd better come home with us," Danny told her gently, "and get something to eat and a little rest."

"Tina is staying," DeeDee countered.

With that Mr. Nicholson spoke up. "I was just going to ask if Tina could go home with you, Danny, and stay there until we come. We'll stay here with the Warrens a while longer."

The girls went back to the Orlis home and helped Kay prepare some sandwiches. They had not thought they could eat at all, but when they sat down at the table they realized how hungry they were. Once their evening meal was over they spent time in prayer, asking God to spare Letitia's life. By ten o'clock both girls had gone to bed in DeeDee's room.

DeeDee awakened when the clock struck eleven and lay there, her eyes open, until after one. When she did go to sleep it was only for a few minutes and she would wake up again. As the night wore on, the icy emptiness within her continued to grow.

The next morning the horrible feeling was still there, gnawing at DeeDee without relief. She thought she was going to be sick.

As she looked around the room, everything seemed to be the same as it was before. She had the same curtains at the window, the same carpet on the floor and the same bedspread on her bed. Nothing inside looked any different, and the sun was shining brightly on the remnants of snow outside her window.

"It all seems like a terrible dream, doesn't it?" she asked Tina weakly.

Tina nodded solemnly in agreement.

Mechanically the two girls dressed and combed their hair, saying little to each other. They still did not feel much like talking. As soon as they went into the kitchen where Danny and Kay were eating breakfast, DeeDee asked if they had heard how Letitia was doing.

Danny explained that he had called but there was no news that the hospital could tell them of.

DeeDee looked wistfully at the clock. "Would we have time to go around by the hospital before Sunday school, Danny?"

"It wouldn't do any good. You can't get in to see her. She won't be having visitors until she's out of danger."

Danny knew how concerned DeeDee was about Letitia and wanted to help her. "We'll call the hospital again after church to find out how she's doing."

They went to Sunday school at the usual time that morning. Everyone was talking about Letitia and the fall she had. There were a dozen rumors, but no one knew anything authoritative until the pastor took a few moments during opening exercises to report on the accident and inform the congregation of Letitia's serious condition.

"I talked with Mr. Warren a few minutes ago," he began. "He tells me that Letitia's condition is unchanged. She is still in intensive care and is listed as being in critical condition."

A gasp went up from the crowd.

"She hasn't regained consciousness and they

don't have any definite knowledge as to the extent of her injuries beyond the fact that she has a broken arm and a broken back."

There was more to his report but DeeDee did not hear him. She had begun to cry again. It was so hard to believe that Letitia, who had been strong and well such a few short hours before, was now lying in a hospital room fighting desperately for her life.

Tina, too, was crying. Del and Doug both saw the tears but they understood. Although neither of them would admit it, they were close to tears themselves.

There was a long session of prayer for Letitia in Sunday school that morning and again in the morning worship service.

The injured girl was on the mind of everyone and it was all DeeDee and Tina could talk about as they went home after church. They reconstructed the events of the afternoon before and speculated once more on Letitia's reasons for going out on the dangerous slope alone. It was such an unusual thing for her to do; so out of character.

"But I don't see why everything has to happen to her," DeeDee said. "I've never seen anyone who has so many bad things come her way. It's just one catastrophe after another."

They stopped to wait for a car that turned in front of them.

"Daddy was talking about the accident on the way down last night. He says he can't understand why she even went over on that slope. She knew everyone else had quit skiing and most of the kids had their skis off and stowed away. She didn't have any good reason for doing what she did."

DeeDee nodded. Everyone had been thinking the same thing. Letitia was not very good on skis and she certainly was not a daring person. She was apt to stay on the easier runs long after she should have been moving up. That would have been more in character. If she had been as good on skis as Tina or some of the other girls, and as excited about skiing, it would have been different. But she did not seem to enjoy skiing all that much. Why would she go off alone on the steepest, most dangerous run in the area?

DeeDee thought and thought about it, but without any plausible explanation. She wondered if she would dare to ask Letitia why she did it, when she began to feel better. She decided it would not be wise to bother her with a lot of questions.

DeeDee ate dinner listlessly, trying to force her thoughts onto different things. The conversation at the table was dull and listless. Nobody mentioned Letitia, but there was no doubt that she was uppermost in the minds of all of them. When they finished eating and had done the dishes DeeDee could stand it no longer. She went into the living room where Danny was sitting and asked about going to the hospital that afternoon.

"Couldn't we go and see how she's doing?" she asked, her voice pleading.

He looked up. "I've already told you that it won't do any good. They aren't allowing anyone except her immediate family in to see her, and even they can only stay a few minutes each hour."

"I know," she said, her voice quavering. "But at least I could be down there for a few minutes. Maybe I could see her folks and talk to them. I could let them know that we're all thinking about her and praying for her and for them, too."

Danny put aside the book he was reading. "The Nicholsons were out at the hospital for a long while with Mr. and Mrs. Warren last night," he said, "but I don't know whether anyone is with them this afternoon." He turned to Kay. "What do you think?"

He didn't really need to ask her, he decided even as he spoke. He knew how tenderhearted she was and how anxious she was to help the distraught parents.

"I feel the same as DeeDee," Kay said. "We can't go in and see Letitia, that's true. And there's really nothing we can do for her right now, but we can let Mr. and Mrs. Warren know that we care."

So Danny drove Kay and DeeDee to the hospital.

The nurse at the desk verified what Danny had already said, that Letitia was in intensive care and only two members of the immediate family could see her at a time, and then only for a period of ten minutes.

"You were one of the girls on the ski trip yesterday, weren't you?" the nurse asked DeeDee.

She nodded.

"If you would like to talk to Mr. and Mrs. Warren for a few minutes, I think it would be all right. They haven't left since their daughter was brought in yesterday afternoon."

She gave them a pass and they went down the long, wide hallway toward the intensive care unit where Letitia was being cared for.

Mrs. Warren came out of the intensive care section and was standing near the door as Danny, Kay, and DeeDee approached. She rushed over to DeeDee quickly and embraced her.

"Oh, I'm so glad you came!" she exclaimed in a guarded whisper.

DeeDee began to cry again, softly. She thought

she had cried so much the past twenty four hours that she would never be able to cry again, but the tears refused to stop.

When she finally had a little better control of herself Mrs. Warren led them a few paces down the hall to a small sitting room where the families and friends of those in intensive care could wait. Danny went over to where Mr. Warren was seated, shook hands with him and sat down by his side. They talked soberly.

"We wanted to come and be with you for a time," Kay told Mrs. Warren quietly.

"I'm so glad you did."

"We're praying constantly for Letitia and for your entire family."

"Oh, thank you."

For a time they sat quietly. It seemed that Mrs. Warren drew strength from the fact that some concerned friends were there with her. Even their quiet presence was comforting.

"How is Letitia doing now?" DeeDee finally asked.

"We got some disturbing news a few minutes ago. The doctor was just in. They're going to operate on her tonight!"

6

God's Promises

DeeDee gasped and for an instant she felt faint. Letitia was going to have an operation! And it was going to be performed on Sunday. That must mean it was an emergency! She must be worse!

"How terrible!" she managed.

Kay, too, was disturbed by the news, although she tried to keep from showing it. "Is this something that just developed?" she asked.

Mrs. Warren shook her head. "I don't know about that for sure. I really don't think so. We asked the doctor how she's doing and he said that she's about the same."

"Then why?" DeeDee choked off the question. If Mrs. Warren wanted them to know she would tell them.

"It's just that they took more X-rays and decided that there are nerves being pinched between the broken vertebrae. The doctor said they had to operate to take the pressure off of them.

What Mrs. Warren could tell them was not too detailed but it did sound serious. It probably meant that if they did not operate, Letitia would be paralyzed or maybe she already was. An operation like that sounded terribly difficult and dangerous.

DeeDee began to tremble violently. If the operation failed it might mean that Letitia would never be able to walk again or she might even die! She cried out to God inwardly, her prayer unspoken in her heart.

They tried to carry on a conversation but that was useless. Nobody was listening to what anyone else said.

Letitia's father had been gone for a short time to talk with the doctor. When he returned, he paused as though undecided whether to join them or not, and finally started in their direction. Mrs. Warren got to her feet.

"How is she?" she asked.

His smile was wan and tired. "About the same." He cleared his throat. "They're taking her into the operating room now."

With that Mrs. Warren started to cry, suddenly, her frail shoulders shaking. Kay put her arms about her tenderly and began to talk to her. With a calm voice she reminded her of God's faithful promise to care for Letitia and for them. Slowly Mrs. Warren's crying ceased. She wiped her eyes with a corner of her handkerchief and even managed a faint smile.

DeeDee listened, too, finding strength and encouragement for her own tortured heart in the promises of God. They had only planned to stay a few minutes but Mrs. Warren seemed to need Kay.

"I'm so glad you came." She paused. "God sent you to be with me this afternoon. Honestly, I don't know what I could have done if it hadn't been for you. I felt as though I couldn't get through this time alone."

"I'm glad that we could come," Kay replied. Then she suggested, "Why don't you come home with DeeDee and me to have something to eat? We only live ten minutes away and your husband can call you if there is anything to report."

Mrs. Warren protested that she was not hungry but Kay suspected that she was afraid to leave the hospital. Mr. Warren finally persuaded his wife to go.

"You'll only be gone about an hour, Margaret," he assured her, "and I doubt if there will be any news in that time. I'll call you at Orlis's as soon as there's any word."

Finally Mrs. Warren was persuaded and went with them. Kay warmed up some left-overs from dinner and fixed a pot of coffee. No one ate very much but the change of atmosphere seemed to relieve the tension a little. After the meal, they read a brief passage from the Bible. The verses spoke of God's strength for those in trouble. Then they spent a short time in prayer.

There had been no word from the hospital, so Mrs. Warren and Kay returned, but DeeDee stayed at home. She called Tina and some of the other Christian girls to arrange to meet them at the church for a special prayer meeting before the evening service. By the time DeeDee and Tina arrived at the church the others were already on their knees, asking God to intercede on Letitia's behalf. It was one of the most wonderful times of prayer DeeDee had ever experienced. Never had God seemed so close to her. And later Tina and some of the others were to express the same feeling. It seemed as though the Lord had been in the very room with them as they cried out to Him.

DeeDee returned from church shortly after eight-thirty. She had no sooner hung up her coat than Kay called to tell them that the operation was over.

"Is she going to be all right?" DeeDee asked quickly.

"We won't know for awhile," Kay said. "The

operation was successful insofar as relieving the pressure on the spinal cord is concerned, but Letitia is very weak and the shock of the operation is great. The surgeon wouldn't even speculate as to when she will be out of danger."

DeeDee returned the phone to its cradle. When she had been at the hospital with Kay and Mrs. Warren she had been so sure they would find out in a few hours whether Letitia would live or not. Now, she learned, the period of waiting had just begun. Even though the operation was over, they still did not know anything very encouraging about her condition. She certainly had not expected anything like this.

"What did she have to say?" Del demanded.

DeeDee shared the news with Del and Doug, then she called Tina to tell her.

Danny and Kay came in after the triplets had gone to bed. DeeDee had not yet gone to sleep. She called to them hopefully as they walked down the hall but they told her there was still no change in Letitia's condition.

While DeeDee was getting ready for school on Monday morning, the telephone rang. She did not dare to let herself imagine who was calling or why.

"It's Letitia's brother," Danny called. "He wants to talk to DeeDee."

"I'll be right there," she answered.

The doctor had said it would probably be several days before the injured girl would be out of danger. Hank's phone call now could only mean one thing. Bad news! She rushed to the phone, afraid to hear what he would say, but afraid not to.

"Hello," she said breathlessly.

"DeeDee?" he echoed. "This is Hank."

"I know."

"You don't sound like yourself."

Suddenly her impatience was sparked. Why did he have to talk about things like that when she wanted to know how Letitia was doing? "How's Letitia? Is she all right?"

"That's why I called you. The doctor was just in to see her. He says that she's making a fine recovery now. He hadn't expected her to improve so rapidly. He feels that she's practically out of danger. He says that she's going to be all right!"

DeeDee's head reeled and for the space of half a minute or more she could not speak. God had answered their prayers! Letitia was going to get well.

Danny and Kay, who were waiting breathlessly to learn the news, saw the relief in DeeDee's face. They, too, relaxed.

"DeeDee! Are you still there?" Hank asked.

Once more she tried to speak, but the words clung for her lips, unvoiced. She had been praying in desperation for Letitia. Yet, somehow, she must not have completely believed that God was going to grant her request.

"Are you all right?" Hank demanded.

"I–" She cleared her throat and tried again. She wanted to assure him that she was, indeed, all right. She wanted to tell him that she was so happy she was speechless, that relief and thanksgiving and praise were all surging through her until she was almost crushed by them. But she could not tell him anything. She could only sob, giving release to all the tension and agony that had been building up within her during the long ordeal.

Kay realized what was happening and went over and gently took the phone from her. "Here," she said. "Let me talk to him."

She explained to the bewildered boy on the line that DeeDee was so relieved she was speechless. Kay suggested that they get together at school instead. She thanked Hank for calling, then she hung up and put an arm about DeeDee's shoulders and guided her to the divan where they sat down together for a few minutes before breakfast.

Although the doctor was well satisfied with the progress Letitia made following the operation, he left her in intensive care for the next several days. By the end of the week, however, she had improved enough so she could be moved to a private room and could have visitors. As soon as that happened Mrs. Warren phoned to tell DeeDee she could go to the hospital for a visit.

"I knew you would want to know," she said.

"That's wonderful!" DeeDee was so happy she was afraid she would start crying again and steeled herself against it.

Mrs. Warren had that same tremulous catch to her voice that had been there since the accident. She, too, was not far from tears.

"I can hardly believe how lucky we've been that things worked out the way they have."

That disturbed DeeDee. It was not luck that Letitia had recovered. God had intervened.

"I don't think it was luck, Mrs. Warren," she said aloud. "Everybody in the church and most of the Christian kids in school were praying for her. It's the Lord who's healing Letitia."

Mrs. Warren did not reply immediately, and when she did it was as though she had not even heard what DeeDee said. "Letitia asked me to call you and tell you that she can have company now.

She said she'd like to have you come up and see her."

"She did?" DeeDee exclaimed. That scarcely seemed possible. Letitia always acted so distant, so much within herself. Being around her, DeeDee could not help feeling that she really did not want, or need friends. Things were better between them than they had been before, but there was still a distance between them.

"I told her how you and Tina and almost everyone else her age in town has been so concerned about her," Mrs. Warren continued. "I think it made a big impression on her. She's asked about you almost every day and has been wondering when you were going to come to see her."

DeeDee's heart soared. This was more than she had even dared to hope for. Letitia wanted her as a friend!

"Do you think it would be all right if Tina comes along?"

"I'm sure Letitia would like that," Mrs. Warren answered.

DeeDee met Tina Nicholson on the walk that morning and they went to school together. Tina agreed to go to the hospital with DeeDee that afternoon in spite of the fact that she could not believe she would be welcome.

"I don't know if she even wants me to come and see her. She's never been very friendly."

"She's never been very friendly to me, either, but her mother says she's been asking for us."

7

Two Visitors

DeeDee and Tina waited anxiously for classes to end that afternoon so that they could go to the hospital and see Letitia Warren. There would not be much time to see her before visiting hours were over, but the main thing was to let her know that they were interested enough in her to come for a visit.

They were hurrying from their homeroom at the close of classes that afternoon when Miss Arvidson, the English teacher, hurried up to them.

"Oh, there you are," she said. "I'm so glad I caught you before you left the building."

They turned back to her uneasily. She was known as one of the stiffest instructors they had. Just having her want to talk to them was enough to be disturbing.

"Is there something wrong?" DeeDee asked.

"Not at all." Her smile was reassuring. "I just happened to remember that you were friends of

Letitia Warren's, and I wondered if you were going to see her before long."

"As a matter of fact, we're on our way to the hospital now. She's out of intensive care and can have company."

"That's good news. And, maybe the news I've go for her will help her, too."

Miss Arvidson went on to tell them that she had been so impressed with Letitia's theme that she entered it in a national contest.

"And that's not all," she continued, excitement tinging her cheeks. "I just heard this morning that her entry is one of the finalists. She has a very good chance of winning one of the prizes."

DeeDee gasped. "She does?" she exclaimed. "That's great!"

"I really think her theme ought to win first," Miss Arvidson interjected, "but I'll have to admit that I'm prejudiced."

As DeeDee thought about the theme her face grew dark. She was happy for Letitia, but she could not see that it was all that good. In fact, she found it most disturbing. The teacher saw the change in DeeDee's features and thought she was jealous of her friend.

"Your theme was good, too, but hers is exceptional," she said. "Letitia has outstanding literary ability."

"It's not that I think my theme should have been entered," DeeDee corrected quickly. "It's just that you're so excited about her theme and I didn't like it that well."

Miss Arvidson was surprised and said so. "You didn't like it?" she echoed. "Why, DeeDee, it almost made me cry."

"It sounded too real to me." DeeDee explained. "I guess that's why I didn't like it."

"But that's the mark of talent. Letitia wrote with her heart."

"Was there anything else you wanted us to tell her?" Tina asked. "Other than the fact that she has a chance of winning the finals?"

"I was going to have you tell her about the contest," Miss Arvidson said, "but I don't think I will now. I think I would like to tell her myself."

DeeDee and Tina left the school building without saying anything to each other and crossed the street in the direction of the lot where Tina had parked her car. Miss Arvidson had only talked with them a few minutes, but it was long enough so the big rush of kids dashing out of the building at the close of the school day was over and the crowd was thinning measurably.

They got into the car and Tina drove to the hospital. They were almost there when she spoke about Letitia's theme for the first time.

"You know, DeeDee, I didn't say anything back at school when Miss Arvidson was talking with us about Letitia's theme, but I agreed with you. I didn't like it either. To tell you the truth, just thinking about it now gives me the creeps."

DeeDee smiled. "I'm glad to hear that somebody agrees with me. I've been wondering if there was something wrong with me because I didn't like it when Miss Arvidson thought it was so wonderful."

Tina shuddered. "I keep thinking about it, even now," she said. "Imagine a girl thinking she was such a burden on her family that she thought killing herself was the solution to their problems. I don't see how anyone could ever dislike herself so much."

"Neither can I," DeeDee agreed.

DeeDee was about to voice her own fear that Letitia might have been writing about herself, sharing her own confused, bewildering feelings, but she decided against it. She did not really know whether that was true or not, or if her concern was born of her own active imagination. Besides, even if it was true she would not want to tell anyone. It would not be fair to Letitia.

The girls reached the hospital half an hour before visiting hours were over for the afternoon. Mrs. Warren was in the room when they got there, but she excused herself and left.

"You don't have to go," DeeDee protested.

"I think I'll take this time to go down and get a cup of coffee," she said. "I'll be back in a few minutes."

Tina and DeeDee had not known for sure what to expect when they went into Letitia's room. They could still see her lying in the snow, her slender figure twisted tortuously. They knew she had been badly injured and had gone through such a serious operation that she had been in critical condition for several days. And they knew she was still very ill and that her body would show the effects of everything that had happened to her. Still, they were not prepared for what they found when they opened the door and stepped into the small, modestly furnished hospital room.

Letitia was lying on her back, encased in a cast from her hips to her neck, holding her body rigid on the narrow bed. She had always been slender but now her face seemed even more thin and drawn. Her cheeks were sallow and colorless.

"Hi," DeeDee said, trying to sound cheerful and

matter-of-fact, as though they were meeting in the hall at school.

"Hello." Letitia's voice trembled uncertainly. She looked up at the two youthful visitors, her eyes dark with emotion.

The girls were afraid she was going to start crying as their eyes met hers. In fact, they were not so sure they could control their own tears.

"How do you feel?" Tina asked her.

"Not too good."

"Your mother said the doctor told her you're coming along fine," DeeDee said.

"That's what they tell me, but they don't know how much it hurts. Most of the time I'm afraid I can't stand it!"

Tina and DeeDee pulled out chairs and sat down close to the bed. They were quiet. There was nothing they could say that would ease the hurt Letitia had to bear. For the space of a minute or more the silence was strained and unnatural.

"Mother told me she thought you would be coming today, but when you didn't get here right after school I was afraid you had decided not to come." The self-pity was creeping into her voice.

"We were going to come over here as soon as school was out," DeeDee said, "but Miss Arvidson stopped us and talked to us."

Something about her tone caused Letitia to realize the teacher had been talking with them about her. Her eyes narrowed.

"She wouldn't ask about me."

"But she did," Tina broke in without thinking. "That was the reason she stopped and talked with us. And wait until you hear what she did with your theme!" She had not intended to mention it. The words popped out, unbidden.

Letitia's head jerked and her gaze bored into Tina. "And exactly what did she do with my theme?" she demanded.

Tina was flustered when she realized that she had told more than she intended. "I'm sorry I said anything about it, Letitia. We weren't supposed to tell."

"What did she do with it?"

"I don't know why I had to open my big mouth!"

Letitia repeated her question again and again, her voice rising each time.

"It wasn't anything bad, if that's what you're thinking," DeeDee told her. "In fact it was something very nice, but we can't tell you what it is. Miss Arvidson wants to come down and tell you about it herself."

They both thought that Letitia would be pleased about the fact that Miss Arvidson had thought enough of her theme to do something special with it, and that she was excited enough to want to come and tell her about it herself. But that was not the case. The hurt deepened in her gaunt face.

"I'm sorry I had to say anything about it, Letitia," Tina told her. "I didn't mean to."

Letitia's lips parted as though she was about to speak but instead she started to cry. DeeDee and Tina tried to comfort her as best they could but that was useless. The more they said and did to get her to stop crying, the harder and more uncontrollably she sobbed. They were on either side of her bed, trying to calm her, when one of the nurses came hurrying in.

"What's going on in here?" she asked sternly.

DeeDee answered her. "We really don't know what happened. "We were just talking with Letitia about one of our teachers when she started to cry and we haven't been able to get her to stop."

The nurse's quick glance was a gesture to move them out of the room. "She's terribly upset. I think you had better leave now."

They both looked helplessly down at their friend and then up at the nurse. They wanted to explain, but how could they? They were bewildered.

"We're sorry Letitia," Tina murmured as they left.

The nurse opened the door and waited until they filed out. Then she closed it behind them decisively.

"What did we do?" DeeDee wanted to know.

Tina shook her head. "I don't have any idea. She seemed upset about her theme, but I don't know why."

Letitia was such a strange person! There was no way of knowing what was going on in her mind or what was going to disturb her. She was not like any of the other girls they knew. They wanted to help her, but that seemed to be impossible. She would not let anyone help.

"Are you going back to see her again?" Tina wanted to know as they drove into the drive at her home.

"I don't know for sure. I wouldn't want to get her that upset again. And besides, do you think the nurses will let us go back?"

DeeDee did not mention to the rest of the family that she and Tina had gone to the hospital to see Letitia that afternoon, but Danny saw that something was wrong and asked her if she was feeling well.

"Oh, sure," she told him. "I feel fine."

"You look as though you're about to cave in," he told her.

"I think she's been upset about Letitia," Kay put in.

DeeDee glanced at her gratefully. She was glad Kay spoke up so she would not have a lot of explanation to make.

She had not even known that Del was going to the hospital that evening until he came home about nine o'clock. He motioned her to the kitchen with a toss of his head.

"What happened between you and Tina and Letitia this afternoon?" he asked, keeping his voice low so the others in the house would not hear.

Her gaze came up slowly to meet his. "Why?"

"Man, was she upset! When I went in there tonight the first thing she did was ask me about you. She wanted to know if you were mad at her."

"It wasn't anything like that at all," DeeDee told him. Now that Del knew about it she was glad to have a chance to talk with him about it. She told him how Miss Arvidson had stopped them to tell them about Letitia's theme and how upset the girl became when Tina let it slip that the teacher had done something special with it. "We thought she was mad at us, the way she acted."

Del understood how the two girls came to be involved. "I can see how you got into it," he said. "I thought it was funny if you went to see her and had some sort of an argument with her. It just didn't sound like you."

"The nurse seems to think it was our fault. Did you tell Letitia we weren't mad at her?" DeeDee wanted to know.

"I told her I knew you weren't, but she wouldn't believe me. You ought to go back up to see her the first chance you get and try to talk some sense into her. She thinks she's killed any chance she's ever had of having you for a friend. She doesn't think you or Tina will want to have anything to do with her anymore."

DeeDee was surprised to learn of Letitia's attitude. She was the one who got upset while they were talking to her. There was nothing they could have done about that. She could not understand how Letitia could even think that would cause them to be angry with her.

"When she thinks about it tomorrow, surely she'll see that we don't have any cause to be angry with her," DeeDee said.

But Del was not so sure about that. He thought Tina and DeeDee should go to the hospital and tell her themselves.

"You wouldn't be mad under circumstances like that," he said, "and neither would Tina or anyone else we know. But Letitia's different. She's different from anyone I've ever known."

DeeDee had to agree with that. Letitia Warren was the strangest person she knew. "But it won't do any good for us to try to go up and talk with her, Del. She was crying so hard when the nurse came in that she thinks we were at fault. She asked us to leave."

"I know, but that was today."

"They probably won't let us in to see her tomorrow or any other time while she's in the hospital either."

His eyes narrowed and his irritation rasped in his voice. "You can try, can't you?"

His tone was so curt and insistent that her temper flamed. After a few moments, however, DeeDee began to realize that he was right. It did not really matter who was at fault. There had been a misunderstanding that had caused a rift between her and Letitia. It had to be straightened out. But how could they manage that when the nurse ordered them out of her room and probably would never let them in again? Neither she nor Tina would be able to get in to see Letitia. She was sure of that.

"Del," she said, calling her brother back as he started for his room. "I would like to go and see

Letitia and get things straightened out. Honestly I would." She went on to tell him again that she was afraid she and Tina could not get in to see Letitia. "Why don't you tell her for me? Tell her that neither of us are mad at her and that we're praying for her every day."

"I'll tell her," he replied, "but I don't think it'll do any good. She wouldn't believe me when I tried to get that across to her tonight."

8

The Unhappy Patient

DEL WENT BACK to the hospital the following day after school and tried to tell Letitia that neither DeeDee nor Tina was angry with her. But she refused to believe him. The more he talked, the more convinced she was that he was not telling her the truth.

"I know you, Del," she said. "You feel bad because this happened and you're just saying they aren't mad to keep me from feeling bad about it."

He shook his head. "I'm telling it to you straight. DeeDee asked me to come here today and tell you what I've just said. She's been afraid that the nurse wouldn't let her and Tina come in to see you."

"I know what they think," the Warren girl continued. "They've decided that I've hurt them all they're going to let me hurt them, so they aren't going to be friends with me anymore. That's the way everything is with me. I don't have any real friends.

Nobody wants to have anything to do with me. That's the way it's been all my life."

Del gave up in despair. He would not have even mentioned the subject to Letitia again but DeeDee kept after him until he agreed to do it.

"You gals have got to get into the hospital and get things straightened out," he told DeeDee in exasperation. "You don't know how upset she is."

"But we can't go and see her, Del!"

"Why not? There isn't any law against it!"

"That's what you think. Tina called the hospital yesterday and asked if we could see Letitia and they refused. They said we were a disturbing influence for her."

"I don't know what they think this mess is," Del blurted. "She's worse now than she's been since you were in there. She won't smile anymore and the last couple of times I've gone in to see her, she's been crying. Something's got to be done and you and Tina are the ones who have to do it!"

"But how? Answer me that!" DeeDee's voice had become shrill.

"Take Kay along with you. She can get you in." Del's voice rose too. "You don't know how bad things are, DeeDee. They're terrible! You've got to go and talk to her!"

Reluctantly DeeDee agreed to go if Kay would

go along with her. She almost hoped her foster mother would refuse, but even as the thought came she knew it would not happen that way. Kay would never refuse any request like that if there was a chance to help someone, and especially a person like Letitia who seemed to need help so desperately.

The following evening they went to the hospital and were given passes to Letitia's room. The supervisor in charge of that wing eyed DeeDee questioningly and muttered that she guessed it would be all right as long as Kay was with her.

Letitia's eyes widened when she saw DeeDee and then they filled with tears. Her voice broke and it was an instant or two before she could speak again. "I didn't think you would ever want to see me again."

"Of course we want to see you." DeeDee went over and took Letitia's hand. "Tina and I would both have been here the day after we came to see you before, but the hospital wouldn't let us in."

Letitia's frail hand was trembling. It was some time before she even tried to talk. "I'm sorry I got so upset about that theme, but when you mentioned that Miss Arvidson had done something with it, I couldn't control myself."

She stopped and swallowed hard. DeeDee knew

she had more to say so she waited until she was ready to continue.

"I'm going to tell you something else, DeeDee, that I didn't think I'd ever tell you. When I wrote that story, I didn't write it to hand in as an English assignment. That was something that just happened. I didn't write it for anyone except you to read, DeeDee!"

"For me?" She couldn't understand what Letitia was talking about. That was even more bewildering than the tears that greeted her on her last visit. "What do you mean?"

"I wrote it for you," she said. "I wanted to tell you those things, but I couldn't. No matter how hard I tried, I couldn't say them. So I wrote about them. Then, when I showed them to you I lost my courage and let you think I'd done the story for the English assignment." She took a deep breath. "You'll probably think I'm terrible, but I lied about it."

DeeDee's bewilderment grew. "But why?" she asked curiously. "Why would you want to tell me the things that were in the theme?"

Letitia stared at her, desperation growing in her eyes. "Don't you understand?" she went on. "That story was true! It's the story of my life!"

DeeDee's head spun. The theme was Letitia's

story, after all! Pity swept over her in great, rolling waves. She looked down at her friend, tears flooding her dark eyes.

Kay did not understand what it was all about, nor did she ask. She had heard enough, however, to know that it was something quite serious. As she stood there quietly she prayed for Letitia, that God would work in her life and give her the strength and courage and wisdom to solve her problems, no matter what they were.

DeeDee and Kay stayed in Letitia's room until visiting hours were over that night. Letitia did not have much to say, but she seemed to be a little more settled when the time came that DeeDee had to go. She took DeeDee's hand and clung to it for almost a minute.

"I wish you didn't have to go," she murmured.

"I'll come back tomorrow if they'll let me in to see you," DeeDee assured her.

DeeDee was able to go back and see Letitia the following evening. The nurse cautioned her about disturbing the patient and then let her go in.

The days wore on endlessly for Letitia. One hour dragged into another and the clock moved with the speed of a calendar. Each hour like a day. She did not know how long she had been in the hospital. Since that fateful afternoon on the ski slope she lost all sense of time. People came in to see her and she wished they would leave, but before they reached the end of the hall she was lonely and restless and wished they would come back.

It was some time three or four weeks following the operation when the night nurse stopped in her room and found her sobbing uncontrollably.

"Say now, Letitia," she began cheerfully, "It's not as bad as all of that, is it?"

There was no answer and the crying did not lessen. The nurse stepped quietly into the room.

"Why, Letitia," she said, "what's wrong? Is something bothering you?"

Finally the girl shook her head but she continued to cry softly.

"Can I do something for you?"

Her tears continued to flow.

"Are you in pain?"

Letitia did not reply.

The nurse thought Letitia was crying from loneliness. "Come to think of it, I don't believe you've had any visitors tonight, have you? Shall I call your mother and have her come down for a while? There's still a little time, and I think we can cheat a little on visiting hours if you would really like to have company. How about it?"

"Oh, no!" Letitia spoke quickly. "Please don't

call her. I can't talk with her tonight. I don't want to talk to anyone!"

The nurse put her hand on the injured girl's forehead, stroking it lightly. She was still not convinced that Letitia was telling her exactly how she felt.

"I'll be all right," the girl murmured.

But Miss Norgren had been trained to read her patients. "Is there someone else you'd like to talk to?" she asked.

Letitia turned away and would not answer. *Why won't this nurse leave me alone? Why does she have to keep after me? Maybe there is someone I would like to talk to, but nobody wants to talk to me,* Letitia thought in a surge of self-pity.

"How about your brother?" the nurse continued. "I could call and have him come in for a little while. Would he do?"

Letitia hesitated. Hank had been up to see her the day before. Talking to him was better than trying to talk to her parents who she thought never understood. But she did not really want to talk to Hank either.

"I know!" The nurse's eyes shone. "Why didn't I think of it before. You'd like to have me call that handsome boyfriend of yours, wouldn't you? Let's see, what was his name again?"

Call Del? Letitia thought she would rather die!

"Oh, no!" she cried. "I don't want to talk to him. Don't you understand? I don't want to see anyone."

The nurse's mouth squeezed to a thin, fine line. "Letitia," she said sternly, "what's wrong?"

Letitia looked up at her plaintively. "I'm just in so much pain tonight. I can't stand it."

Miss Norgren was surprised. "You shouldn't be," she said. "The surgery was over a month ago. You ought to be feeling good by now."

"That's what I hear all the time. So I feel great! I'm supposed to be ready to get out of here and go skiing again! Everybody else knows what I should do and how I should feel. How I really feel doesn't matter at all!"

"Have you told the doctor about your pain?" the nurse asked.

"What good would that do? He's just like the rest of you."

Miss Norgren ignored the sarcasm. "I'll call him and tell him that you're not resting well." She made a notation on her records.

"You don't have to bother him, do you?"

"He has left word for us to phone him immediately if there are any problems with any of his patients."

"There isn't any problem. I've had so much pain the last three or four nights that I haven't slept much. I wondered if I could have another of those sleeping pills."

Miss Norgren studied her narrowly. "You've had sleeping pills the last three or four nights. Did they help you?"

"I thought maybe I could get something a little stronger tonight."

"I see." The nurse went over her chart carefully. "I'll be back in a minute."

Letitia had tried to read Miss Norgren's face to see if she was sympathetic. *I don't know why nurses are so stubborn,* she thought. *Weren't they hired to see that their patients have what they want? Well, in a few more days it will be all over and I won't be causing my folks or anybody else any more trouble.*

Letitia's lips trembled and she steeled herself against the tears. To cry now would risk everything. Miss Norgren seemed suspicious already.

Letitia's eyes were closed when the nurse came back into the room with two small white tablets and a glass of water.

"Here you are," she said crisply. "I hope these help you to sleep better."

Letitia opened her eyes triumphantly.

"Oh, thank you. I know they will."

She expected Miss Norgren to stand right there while she took the pills, or pretended to. That was what all the other nurses had done and she had had a terrible time making them believe she took the pills.

As soon as Miss Norgren left the room. Letitia pulled a small pill envelope out of the cast on her arm and dropped the pills in with the others she had been hoarding. The next night, or the next, she would be ready. And this time she would not fail!

9

The Nurse's Discovery

LETITIA was putting the tiny envelope back into the opening in the palm of her cast when Miss Norgren came striding in. She went directly up to the head of the bed, towering angrily over the girl who lay there. Letitia's stomach squirmed miserably.

"What are you doing?" Miss Norgren asked accusingly.

"I'm going to try to get some sleep if this pain doesn't keep bothering me," Letitia answered, trying to sound hurt and put upon.

"What were you dong with that little envelope," the nurse persisted.

Letitia's cheeks paled and she knew her lips were blue and trembling. She said nothing.

"Please give it to me." Miss Norgren's voice was quiet but insistent.

"No!"

"Letitia, give it to me," she repeated. "I saw you

put those tablets into an envelope instead of taking them, Letitia."

"That's not true!"

Miss Norgren had no difficulty in pulling the pill envelope from the cast. Letitia was still too weak to struggle.

"Just as I thought!" the nurse exclaimed.

Surprisingly, Letitia did not cry. She was too hurt, too shamed and drained of emotion to find energy for tears. The nurse's entire manner changed. Her anger drained away, swept by compassion that flooded over her.

"I don't know what your problem is," she said, "but I do know that this isn't the answer."

She went on to tell the distraught girl that she suspected something was wrong when she asked about a sleeping pill again, so she had called the doctor and checked with him. He decided that she should be given a couple of small sugar pills and watched to see what she did with them.

"You mean they, they weren't even real?" Shame tortured her. "Why couldn't you let me do it? I'm no good to my parents or anyone else! I don't see why you had to be so nosey!"

"I can understand how you feel toward me right now," the nurse continued, "but in a few days I hope you'll feel differently. Don't you see, Letitia? We want to help you!"

The silence was long and painful.

"Will my folks have to know?" she asked, at last. "I've hurt them so much already I won't be able to stand it if they find out about this!"

Miss Norgren did not reply immediately. "That is a question the doctor will have to answer, but I'm sure your parents would be understanding. They want you to be well and happy."

"That's not it!" Letitia cried in anguish. "That's not it, at all!"

The doctor came in just then, talked with her for twenty minutes or so and left instructions for Miss Norgren at the nurse's station to go through Letitia's personal things that were close to her bed.

"We must be sure that she doesn't have some more medication stashed away somewhere."

The nurse nodded her understanding.

"And if she doesn't sleep?" she asked.

He scribbled on the girl's chart. "I'm leaving instructions for a mild sedative. She's terribly concerned about having her parents find out about this. I promised her that I wouldn't call them until morning."

When he was gone the nurse went back to Letitia's room. The doctor had told her to keep a close watch on the girl, but he needn't have done so. She was determined to help her however she could.

"How are you feeling now?" the nurse asked Letitia.

"Miserable."

"Would you like some hot tea or a coke?"

The girl's gaze met hers. "You must think I'm a terrible person!"

"I think you're a very lovely, confused girl and I want to help you all I can."

Letitia did not move. "You don't really mean that. You're just like everyone else. Nobody cares about me!"

"That's not true. You have lots of friends. I've seen them come up here to visit you."

"That's because Hank or someone asked them to be nice to me."

As Miss Norgren talked with her patient she realized her own helplessness and repeated the question she asked earlier.

"Would you like to talk to someone?"

"And tell them what a fool I made of myself?" Letitia echoed.

"When I was your age I had one very special friend. We were so close I could tell her anything and she would understand."

Letitia thought of DeeDee. If there was anyone

she knew who would listen to her and not tell it all over church and at school it was DeeDee.

"Why don't you let me call someone?"

She stepped over to the telephone on the small table beside her bed.

"What about those two girls who visit so often?" Miss Norgren asked. "Wouldn't you like to see them?"

At first Letitia did not answer. She was not sure she knew Tina well enough to share anything with her. Besides, because she was rich and did not seem to have any problems, Letitia was afraid she would not be understanding. Finally, looking up at the nurse, the girl spoke so softly she was barely heard.

"Yes, I think I would like to talk with DeeDee Davis for a little while, but she wouldn't want to talk with me."

"You don't know that."

"She's probably too busy, anyway."

Miss Norgren reached for the phone. "Now, you just give me her number and we'll find out right away."

It was fairly late when the nurse called the Orlis home and DeeDee was working on her American history. She took the message thoughtfully. When Kay came into the room, DeeDee was still standing by the phone.

"What was that all about?"

DeeDee frowned as she returned the phone to its cradle. "One of the nurses at the hospital called and said that Letitia wants to see me."

"Tonight?"

"That's what I asked, too. It's past visiting hours and they've been so strict about having everyone leave on time before. But the nurse said it was important that I come. She's going to arrange for me to get a pass."

"That is strange." Kay had difficulty understanding why the nurse would want DeeDee to come down after hours. There must be some good reason, but she could not quite figure out what it could be.

It only took DeeDee a few minutes to put her books away and get ready to go to the hospital. Her own apprehension grew. At first she thought Letitia must have developed some sort of complications, but that really did not make sense. In a case like that the doctor would call her parents. Then, too, Letitia was getting along so well lately. Everyone said it was just a matter of time until she was out of the hospital and back in school.

At the door she hesitated momentarily, the car keys in her hand. She could go alone, but she decided, suddenly, that she wanted Kay with her.

She went back and asked her foster mother to go too. Kay was happy to go but she told DeeDee she would wait in the hall. "I'm not sure that Letitia would want both of us. If she's having some sort of problem and has decided she wants to share it with you, she probably won't like it if I'm along."

"I might need you," DeeDee said. "Besides, Letitia likes you. I'm sure she won't mind."

DeeDee did want Kay along to help her talk with Letitia, that was true. And Letitia did like Kay. She had told DeeDee a number of times that she wished her own mother was half as understanding and as easy to talk to as Kay was. But there was another reason. She found going to the hospital disturbing. She really didn't want to go and see Letitia alone.

When DeeDee reached her friend's room Kay waited in the hall and the nurse, who was standing beside Letitia's bed, left quietly. Letitia's eyes filled with tears. DeeDee reached down and took her hand.

"Hi."

"I didn't think you would come," Letitia began.

"You should know better than that. I'd come see you anytime." DeeDee took a deep breath. "Is there something wrong?"

Letitia wiped the tears away and fought for control.

"Did the nurse tell you anything?"

"Only that you wanted to talk to me."

"She didn't stop you in the hall and say anything?"

"No. What is it Letitia?" DeeDee asked brokenly. "What's wrong?"

A tense silence hung between them.

"I don't know why, but Miss Norgren insisted that I call someone, and the only person I could think of was you."

"I'm glad you felt you could call me, Letitia."

"You're going to think I'm terrible!"

"No, I won't!"

"But you don't know! *You don't know!*" It was only with great effort that she was able to keep from crying again. Her voice caught in her throat and for a moment or two she was unable to continue.

Once she was able to talk again, the words tumbled out, one crowding upon another until DeeDee could scarcely understand her. She told her about the pills and how Miss Norgren had caught her hoarding them.

Shocked, DeeDee started to cry, but only for an

instant. She prayed for strength to keep control of herself so she could help her friend.

"Why, Letitia?" she asked.

She went on to relate some of the things she had shared with DeeDee before. She told her how unhappy she had been at home, how she had always been sick, and that there were so few kids at school and church who really liked her. Nobody cared whether she was around or not. It was not that she was disliked. They just ignored her.

"It seems that one problem has piled on another, lately," she went on, "until I thought I would explode. And then Daddy lost his job again!"

"That would have been bad enough," she continued, "but the fighting and bickering between my parents has made me more miserable than ever.

"You were the one who asked me to go to the ski party," she said, "and I know you thought I came along to have a good time, if I could, but that wasn't it at all. I had another reason for going."

DeeDee stared at her. "You did?"

"That skiing accident wasn't really an accident at all," she explained. "I was so fed up with everything that I thought I might as well do something drastic and end all of my unhappiness and all the trouble I've caused everyone else."

DeeDee was shocked.

"I knew the slope I went on was too steep for me. I hadn't been skiing for a year and I wasn't nearly good enough to try that run. I knew I would fall and thought that would be the end of everything for me. I thought that was going to solve my parents' problems too. But I failed at that just like I failed tonight! That's the story of my life! I'm a failure at everything!"

10

A Friend's Counsel

DEEDEE WAS ASTONISHED at the things Letitia was telling her. In some ways it embarrassed her, as though her friend was revealing too much of herself. At times she felt like putting out her hand to stop the flow of words. But somehow it seemed that the girl needed to pull it all out and let someone other than herself know about it.

"I've felt this way for a long time," she continued, "and I tried and tried to get up courage enough to tell you about it, but I couldn't. Every time I tried, the words would choke in my throat and I couldn't say anything. I finally decided to write it in a story and let you read it, but I was too embarrassed to let you know why I'd done it so I pretended I wrote it for Miss Arvidson's English class."

"Was that the reason you got so upset when Tina let it slip that Miss Arvidson had done something special with your theme?" DeeDee asked.

Letitia nodded. "I felt as though I'd been betrayed. I was afraid everyone in town would know the truth."

DeeDee could understand that now. The things Letitia had done began to make sense. Her mind was spinning from her new knowledge. Right then she had to try to think of something that would be of help to her distraught friend. While she was mentally searching for some Bible verses, Letitia spoke once more.

"You think I'm terrible, don't you?" she asked.

DeeDee did not speak. She did not think Letitia was terrible at all, although she had tried to do a terrible thing. But she did not know what to say to help her. It was all so confusing.

"To tell you the truth, I think I'm awful," Letitia went on. "I'm so ashamed I could just—" She could not finish.

There was a long pause as DeeDee prayed silently.

"Dear God, help me to find the words to comfort Letitia and to make her see that You want to help her. I don't know what to say to her or what to do."

While DeeDee was still praying, Letitia interrupted her thoughts.

"Like I said, I've been nothing but a problem to

my family all my life. They'd all be better off without me."

"That's not true," DeeDee tried to assure her. "God had a purpose in sending you to live with your father and mother. He permitted these things to happen for a definite purpose, even though I can't tell you what that purpose is. I can tell you that He'll help you to have the strength and courage you need, even for a time like this."

Letitia's eyes rounded. She had wanted to share her troubles with DeeDee but she had never expected to hear her say anything like that.

"But you don't know what it's like," she protested. "You've never had to go through anything like this! You've had things easier. You've lived a good, happy life."

"I haven't had to go through exactly the same things that you have, Letitia," DeeDee tried to explain, "but don't think I've had it easy. My mother and father both were drowned in the same accident when Del and Doug and I were just little kids. It wasn't easy for us then and there are a lot of times when it isn't easy for us now. But we found out that God can, and does, give us the strength we need to face what comes."

DeeDee went on to tell how terrible she felt after the tragedy in Guatemala in which her parents lost their lives. She told Letitia that it seemed as though she was completely alone and that if God had loved them He would not have taken away both her parents.

"But through it all I learned that God does care and that He helps us and gives us the courage we need to live day by day. I found out that I could put my trust in Him and know that He would help me. Sure, sometimes I have questions and doubts and problems, but I learned what it is to live the faith a lot of people only talk about. He'd help you too, Letitia, if you would allow Him to."

As she continued to talk, the lines in her friend's face began to soften. For the first time she began to see that there was help for her, too; that she could ask God and know that He would help her the same way that He helped DeeDee.

"But I've gone too far," she murmured, a desperate longing taking hold of her. "Don't you see? I actually tried to take my life. God would never forgive me for what I tried to do on the ski run and what I was planning to do up here."

"God is bigger than that," DeeDee said. "He forgave Paul and he was a murderer. He actually killed Christians. God says in the Bible that He will forgive us and He doesn't lie. You can take care of everything right now, if you want to."

There was a long, pained silence. Letitia wanted to believe DeeDee and put her trust in Jesus the way she had, but it was so hard for her to realize that He loved her enough to forgive her for everything. Oh, she had accepted Him as her Saviour a long time ago, but lately she had grown so far away from Him. She had stopped trusting anyone, even God.

"He wouldn't give me the same kind of peace He's given you. He wouldn't, would He, DeeDee?"

"Of course, He will. All you have to do is let Him work in your heart."

"But you haven't done all the terrible things that I've done."

"God doesn't care about such things, Letitia," she replied. "I don't mean He doesn't care. He does care about our sinning. What I mean is that He doesn't care how bad our sins have been. If we come to Him and ask His forgiveness, and are really sincere, He'll forgive us no matter what we've done."

Silence hung heavily for a moment.

"Won't you ask Him to forgive you now, Letitia?"

The injured girl stared beyond DeeDee and into space. It seemed to DeeDee that Letitia would never speak. She was about to continue herself when the other girl's lips parted.

"It wouldn't do any good for me to try to trust God to take care of my life." Her voice quavered. "I couldn't possibly live a good enough life to deserve His help."

"Neither could I. But one of the wonderful things about God's grace is that we don't have to earn His help. All we have to do to get it is to trust Him for it."

"I can't go on living the way I have been," she blurted. "I've been telling lies and you know what my life has been like."

"God knows, too," DeeDee assured her. "He wants to help you clean it up and to come back to Him."

"But I can't keep from doing those things. I've tried!"

DeeDee could understand Letitia's frustration if she had been trying to live the Christian life under her own power.

"And you failed, of course. Everybody does. You can only be a Christian with God's power."

Letitia was quiet for a minute. What DeeDee said was not new. She had heard the same thing in church and young people's. She felt foolish because she had to learn the hard way.

"You make it sound so simple though, DeeDee," she said at last.

"It is simple. It's as simple as it was when you first confessed your sin and accepted the Lord Jesus Christ as your Saviour. And in one way you don't have to do anything yourself. In another way you have everything to do with it."

Letitia moistened her parched lips. "What do you mean?"

"You've got to turn your life over to God and allow Him to change you in any way He wants to. You've got to let Him take away your self-pity and your inferiority feelings."

"But I've done such awful things. I've wronged so many people." Tears filled her eyes once more. "I've done so much I shouldn't have done that I don't even know where to start."

DeeDee wasn't quite sure she knew how to guide her friend, but there was only one way she knew of to get back into fellowship with God. She had heard the pastor preach about it.

"The first thing you've got to do is to confess your sin to God and ask His forgiveness for all your doubts and failures," she said. "You may have to go to some people and ask their forgiveness," she said quietly. "God will talk to you about that. But first He will forgive you and give you peace. Then you can expect Him to take hold of your life and make it over to suit Him."

Letitia still had more questions. She wanted to know if God would actually forgive her for the attempt she made to take her own life, and if He would help her not to be so despondent and unhappy.

DeeDee was amazed that she found the answers to her friend's questions and was able to explain them so Letitia could understand. She realized that God was helping her.

At last her overwrought friend was ready to pray. Letitia closed her eyes and asked God to forgive her and to help her face the problems that came her way. When she finished, DeeDee prayed, thanking God for meeting Letitia's needs.

When they finished praying, DeeDee took her New Testament from her purse and read a few verses. She was still reading when the nurse looked in. Miss Norgren seemed flustered at the sight of the Bible, but she said nothing. DeeDee thought the nurse wanted her to leave and got quickly to her feet.

"It's getting late. I should run."

"There's no hurry," Miss Norgren told her, studying her patient's face. She noticed the change in Letitia. She looked calm and settled.

"I really should be going," DeeDee said again. "I've got classes tomorrow and I still have more math problems to finish."

Letitia grasped her friend's hand and for a moment held her tightly. "You will come back and see me tomorrow, won't you?"

"Of course I will," DeeDee replied. "I'm glad I could come tonight, Letitia. I'll see you tomorrow."

With that DeeDee and Kay left the hospital. The nurse followed them some distance from the girl's room.

"I don't know what you said in there, DeeDee," Miss Norgren said, "but I never saw such a change come over anyone so quickly. Letitia has been through a traumatic emotional experience and now she seems relaxed and settled."

"Thank you for calling us," Kay said.

Neither Kay nor DeeDee said anything until they were outside once more. Then Kay turned to her foster daughter.

"Things must have gone all right in there this evening, according to what Miss Norgren said just now."

DeeDee nodded. "I didn't know what to say to her, but God worked in her heart. She came back to Him tonight."

"Can you tell me about it?" Kay asked.

"I'm sure Letitia wouldn't mind if I share it with you. I know you won't say anything to anyone else about it."

"If you feel you shouldn't, don't tell me."

"Oh, no. I've got to talk to someone about it."

As they drove home DeeDee poured out the entire story of Letitia's unhappy life, right up to the incident at the ski party and the incident with the sleeping pills.

"She had been pretending to be in pain and couldn't sleep," she said, "so the nurses would give her some pills for it. She had saved them and just about had enough so she could take her life."

"How terrible!" Kay murmured.

"If God hadn't worked so that she was willing to confide in me I don't know what would have happened. The next time she tried, she might have been successful."

"I was thinking that myself."

"I get cold chills when I realize that I almost gave up on Letitia!" DeeDee said. "I had decided there was nothing I could do to help her and I wasn't even sure that I wanted to be her friend anymore." DeeDee was crying again but she scarcely noticed the tears.

"That ought to show us we should never give up on anyone we're praying for."

DeeDee paused thoughtfully. "I don't know why God used me to talk to Letitia, but I'm glad He did. I've never been so happy or felt so close to Him in all my life!"

11

Letitia's Change

In the hospital room Miss Norgren took Letitia's pulse, talking quietly with her as she did so. The girl was more calm and relaxed than she had been at any time since she came into the hospital. It was incredible.

"How do you feel?" Miss Norgren questioned.

"Better, thanks."

"That's good. I'm so glad you let me call Dee-Dee. I don't know what she said or did, but whatever it was, it was the best medicine you could have had. You act as though you're a different person."

"It wasn't really DeeDee, although she helped," Letitia told her. "I'd like to tell you what happened, if you have time to listen."

"I'd like that." Miss Norgren pulled up a chair and sat down.

"I've been a Christian since I was real young," Letitia began, "but I felt so sorry for myself that

I thought God didn't love me. It wasn't long until I quit trusting Him the way I should and my life got all messed up. I lied and did a lot of other things that were wrong."

"We all do," Miss Norgren said uneasily.

"And I've hurt a lot of people who've been trying to help me. But tonight DeeDee helped me to see that I couldn't blame my personal problems for my sin. We prayed and I asked God to forgive me and He did. Now I've got to make things right with the people I've hurt so I can live the way God wants me to live."

Miss Norgren drew herself erect. "That's fine, Letitia. I'm glad religion helped you," she said awkwardly.

"It wasn't religion, Miss Norgren. It was Christ. He's the One who saved me and forgave my sins."

The nurse had nothing to say. She felt very uneasy and lightly patted the girl's hand. Letitia's words upset her strangely.

The change that had come into Letitia Warren's life continued to show itself in the days that followed. Before she committed her life completely to Christ, she had been despondent and morose most of the time. She had complained about the pain, the food, and the nursing care. It had reached the point where none of the nurses would enter her room if they could avoid it.

Suddenly, however, everything was different. She seldom complained, and she joked with the nurses as they came in, even though pain was still as bad as before. Her closer relationship to Christ had not changed that. She was still concerned about whether she would be able to walk again once she was out of the cast, although the doctor had assured her she would. But now the way she reacted to the discomforts and loneliness associated with being in the hospital was so different that everyone was talking about it.

"I don't think I've ever seen such a change in a person," Miss Norgren commented to another nurse. "Frankly, I hated to take care of her before, but it's a pleasure to go into her room now."

"I know," one of the nurse's aides said, picking up Letitia's chart and looking at it thoughtfully. "And there hasn't been that much change in her physical condition."

"I'm sure she's no more comfortable than she was before," another nurse said. "The only thing I don't like about her is her constant talk about her religion. I'm glad it helped her, but really—"

Miss Norgren nodded. She had thought she was the only one who was disturbed by the way their patient talked about Jesus Christ. She made a notation on another chart before looking up. "There are times when she makes me wonder what it would be like to believe like she does. She certainly makes it appealing."

The other nurse laughed. "Watch out, Norgren, or she'll get to you."

The aide turned quickly and went down the hall in response to a light above the door of one of the rooms. She supposed there was something to what Miss Norgren was saying. She had talked with Letitia more than anyone else. In a way she felt more deeply involved in her tremendous unhappiness and the attempt on her life. She supposed that was because she had been the one who discovered it.

And Miss Norgren had seen more vividly how much the girl's faith in Jesus Christ was helping her. Everyone else talked about how good it was that she had been able to get hold of herself. But Miss Norgren realized that that was not really what had happened. She knew it was Letitia's faith.

Miss Norgren was sure she did not want to become a Christian. She had stopped attending church years before because she believed religion is a crutch. It was alright for weaker people, but she had no need for it. But Letitia's case seemed different and the more she thought about it, the more interested she became.

Miss Norgren found opportunities to go into Letitia's room often.

"And how are you this evening?" the nurse asked one night after visiting hours.

"Wonderful!" was Letitia's sincerely happy reply.

Miss Norgren realized she could not have honestly answered that way even though she did consider herself a reasonably happy, well-adjusted individual.

"Maybe I ought to get religion, too, if it will do as much for a person as it has for you," the nurse commented, half joking.

"Not religion," Letitia corrected her again. "It's Jesus Christ who works miracles in people. He can help people solve all their problems by giving them a new life and helping them put aside the old one. You know that He did that for me."

The nurse squirmed uncomfortably. She had seen Christ work.

"I don't know what would have happened to me if I hadn't come back to Christ and turned my life over to Him," Letitia said seriously. "I just might have accomplished what I tried to do, and if that had happened I would have completely ruined the lives of everyone in my family. That's all over now, though. Whatever happens I can put my trust in Jesus Christ to give me strength and courage and the help I have to have to face life."

Miss Norgren edged toward the door.

"I'd like to stay here and talk with you, but I have other patients. I have to check on them."

"Will you come back in a little while?" Letitia coaxed.

"I think I'll be able to stop in a little later," the nurse replied, planning to just visit for a minute or two.

She had a dinner date with a popular young bachelor at the fanciest night spot in the area. The last thing she wanted was to become involved in a discussion on Christ and sin.

At the end of her rounds, Miss Norgren stopped back at Letitia's room.

"I'm so glad you came back," Letitia said, reaching out and taking the nurse's hand. "I've got something to show you."

"I can only stay a minute," the nurse countered lamely.

"This won't take very long. Look in that drawer and get that little booklet that asks if you've ever heard of the four spiritual laws."*

**Four Spiritual Laws* (San Bernardino, Calif.: Campus Crusade for Christ Internat., 1965).

Miss Norgren did so. "Can you hold it over here so I can read along with you? See, first it asks if you know that God loves you and that He has a wonderful plan for your life."

"I can't say that I've ever thought about it," Miss Norgren replied. She tried to sound indifferent, although the thought intrigued her. She read the Bible verse that told of God's love, and the one that told of His plan for her life. She knew the first verse. She had learned it as a little girl.

" 'For God so loved the world, that He gave His only begotten Son, that whoever believes in Him should not perish, but have eternal life' (John 3:16)."

She could not remember ever having heard the second verse. "I came that they might have life, and might have it abundantly" (John 10:10).

Now she began to understand what had made Letitia so different. Her beliefs were real to her. This surprised Miss Norgren because she always had had the idea that Christianity was just a long list of don'ts.

"Wouldn't you like to have the life God offers you, Miss Norgren?" Letitia persisted. "Wouldn't you like to have the same happiness I have?"

Mechanically the nurse turned the page without answering.

The injured girl went on to explain the second law, that people are unhappy and miss the abundant life because they are sinful and separated from God.

This was a new thought to Miss Norgren, and the Bible verses Letitia quoted could not be explained away. There was even a chart that showed how sinful man was separated from God by a great chasm. She began to see that no matter how hard man worked to reach God, he could never do it.

"It would be terrible if it ended there, but it doesn't. The third spiritual law is that Jesus Christ is God's answer for man's need. Through Him you can have forgiveness." Letitia went on to tell how God sent His Son, Jesus Christ, to die on the cross in our place and to be the way between God and man.

"That sounds simple enough," Miss Norgren observed. She closed the little booklet and put it in her pocket. "I'll read this over again sometime. I've really got to hurry. I've got an important date."

"But you can't stop there!" Letitia added excitedly. "It won't help you at all if you don't go any further than that."

Reluctantly Miss Norgren took the booklet from her pocket and turned to the fourth law.

Letitia read it aloud, " 'We must individually receive Jesus Christ as Savior and Lord; then we can know and experience God's love and plan for our lives.' " She went on to quote the Bible verses. " 'But as many as received Him, to them He gave the right to become children of God, even to those who believe on His name' (John 1:12). 'For by grace you have been saved through faith; and that not of yourselves, it is the gift of God; Not as a result of works, that no one should boast' (Ephesians 2:8-9)."

Miss Norgren's hands were trembling. Letitia knew she had understood.

"Wouldn't you like to put your trust in Jesus Christ so you can have the abundant life God wants you to have?" she asked.

The nurse nodded silently.

"Then, why don't we pray together right now?"

They both bowed their heads to pray. Letitia Warren led her first soul to Christ! A great joy swept over her.

12

First on the List

Hank Warren had been concerned about Letitia because she was so withdrawn and had such problems making friends with the kids at school, but he had even more difficulty understanding the change that had come over her so suddenly. She seemed to have become a totally new person since she came back to Jesus Christ and experienced complete forgiveness.

He was amazed that she could now accept her condition without rebellion. She was still in the same hospital bed and her body was encased in the same ugly, uncomfortable cast. She was even suffering from the same pain. But there was such a difference.

She did not complain about the accident anymore and she actually seemed happy. And seeing her and listening to her tell what her new peace in God was doing for her, disturbed him so much he had a hard time sleeping at night or keeping his mind on his school work.

His folks were confused by the change that had come into her life, too, but he had not planned to say anything about it to them. The subject slipped out when he was talking to his dad.

"What's with Letitia lately?" Hank asked.

Mr. Warren squinted across the table at him. "What do you mean?"

"She talks about religion all the time and she's so happy now that everybody wants to go in and visit her. I don't get it."

"Neither do I, but I'm not complaining. Your mother and I have been so worried about her since the accident that we haven't known what to do. We've been grateful for the way she's been the last week or so."

Hank was not sure he agreed. He felt uncomfortable when he visited her and he was confused and embarrassed when his friends mentioned that they had gone to see her.

Actually, Letitia had given Hank her testimony just as she did when anyone commented on the wonderful change that had come over her. He was embarrassed to think of her "preaching" to everyone who visited her.

Hank decided to go over to the snack shop. There was always a gang of his friends there.

Sure enough, a bunch of the kids he knew were sitting around one of the tables when he got there. As soon as they saw him, the conversation stopped. He noticed that immediately and it bothered him.

"Hey, Hank, come on over."

He did so, mechanically, dreading what was sure to come next.

"Hi." He had to force out the greeting.

"Sit down. We want to talk to you," one of the boys said.

"What's the deal with Letitia?" his old girl friend, Betty, wanted to know.

Hank scooted into the booth, his cheeks blazing. "What do you mean?"

Betty twisted in the seat to stare at him. "Is that religion she talks about for real?"

"Why don't you ask her?" he replied.

"I did, but the others won't believe what she told me. She said it's the most wonderful thing that ever happened in her life."

No one was watching Betty as she spoke. Their eyes were fixed on Hank.

"I don't see how religion can make such a change in a person," one of the guys said seriously. "Is that what it is, Hank? Is it religion that makes her so happy in spite of everything that happened to her?"

He had difficulty in answering. "Search me."

"It can't be. It's got to be more than that." There was no contempt in his voice—only concern.

"That's what I've been trying to tell you," Betty continued, "But you won't listen. Letitia says it isn't religion that helped her. She says it's because she has a personal relationship with Jesus Christ. She trusts Him to help her bear the pain and be happy in spite of a broken back."

Everyone was quiet for a minute.

"I don't get it. But if it's for real, it's worth having," Betty added.

Hank Warren's eyes were wide and staring. The words struck at his consciousness forcefully, hammering into him. He had not imagined that his friends would be so impressed by Letitia. It was enough to shake anybody!

He left the snack shop presently and made his way to his car. He had to sort out his thoughts so he drove around for a while.

It was that DeeDee Davis who caused all this, he decided. Letitia had been reasonable about religion until she started talking to her. And the worst of it was that he had been the one who urged DeeDee to befriend his sister.

Hank turned in the direction of the hospital without quite knowing why. If he had realized what DeeDee was like he never would have put her on Letitia's trail.

Well, there was one thing sure, he was determined not to let her get him roped into it. He turned the car around and headed for home. Thinking that Letitia's "religious kick" would last only a week or two, he decided to stay away from the hospital until she settled down and stopped "preaching."

DeeDee visited Letitia practically every day. It was exciting to go into her hospital room now that she was a vibrant, victorious Christian. It seemed something thrilling was always happening, like the time Hank's friends came to visit.

Letitia had the opportunity to tell them how they could have the same happiness she had by confessing their sin and putting their trust in Jesus. She told DeeDee all about it in detail, her eyes shining with anticipation.

"Nobody made a decision for Christ," she related, "but they said they want to come back and talk to me again. I'm praying that the next time they'll give their hearts to Jesus."

"I'll pray for them, too," DeeDee promised.

"Will you? That's wonderful!"

The next day when DeeDee went in to see her, Letitia had a long prayer list made out.

"As long as you're praying, I thought I'd ask you to pray for these, too. I'm claiming them for Christ, like the pastor suggested when he came to see me."

DeeDee looked at the list. Hank's name was at the top. For some reason she was surprised at that. But she shouldn't have been, she decided. Hank had been so concerned about Letitia a few months before. Now the situation was reversed. Only there was a big difference. Letitia had something now that would help Hank. He only had concern and was really helpless to do anything for her.

Hank was so self-assured that for an instant she doubted whether even Letitia's faith could reach him. Then trust flooded over her in a great, warm wave. It might take a long while for Hank to respond, but that really made no difference. She knew that one day Hank Warren would follow his sister and make a decision for Christ.

DeeDee bowed her head and thanked God for the wonderful way He had worked in Letitia's life. DeeDee thanked Him, too, for the small part He permitted her to play. How grateful she was to know Letitia and claim her as a friend.